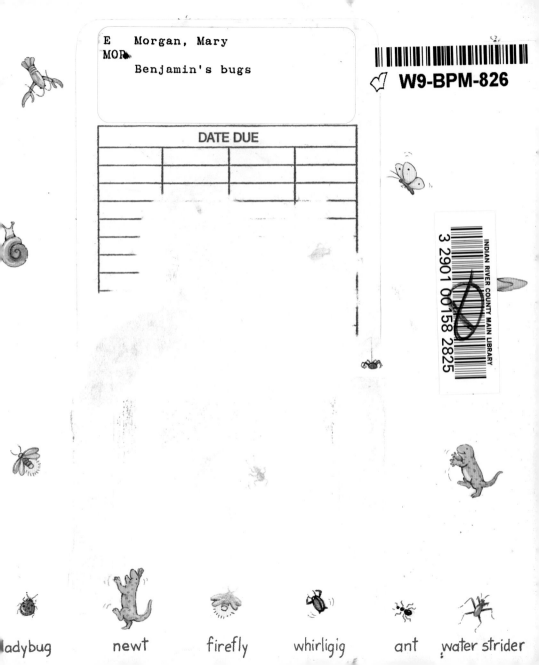

ladybug   newt   firefly   whirligig   ant   water strider

Benjamin's Bugs

by Mary Morgan

Bradbury Press · New York

Maxwell Macmillan Canada · Toronto
Maxwell Macmillan International
New York · Oxford · Singapore · Sydney

Bradbury Press
Macmillan Publishing Company
866 Third Avenue
New York, NY 10022

Maxwell Macmillan Canada, Inc.
1200 Eglinton Avenue East
Suite 200
Don Mills, Ontario M3C 3N1

Macmillan Publishing Company is part of the Maxwell Communication
Group of Companies.

The text of this book is set in 20-point Souvenir Light.
The art is rendered in watercolor.
Book design by Julie Quan
Printed in the United States of America on recycled paper
First edition
10 9 8 7 6 5 4 3 2 1
LIBRARY OF CONGRESS CATALOGING-IN-PUBLICATION DATA
Morgan, Mary, date.
Benjamin's bugs / by Mary Morgan.—1st ed.
p.   cm.
Summary: Curious Benjamin Porcupine has a series of misadventures
while out walking with his mama.
ISBN 0-02-767450-9
[1. Porcupines—Fiction.   2. Behavior—Fiction.]   I. Title.
PZ7.M8254Be   1994
[E]—dc20   93-22911

For my parents
and my son, Dylan

One sunny day Benjamin
Porcupine and his mama
went for a walk.

Mama walked slowly
down the path while
Benjamin stopped to
talk to an ant....

Then he stopped to
roll and tumble....

Then he stopped to
taste a dandelion....

Then Benjamin stopped
to climb a tree.

When Benjamin was way up in the tree, he looked around. He did not know how to get down! Benjamin called, "Oh, help! Mama!"

"Come down, Benjamin,"
his mama said. He
jumped into her arms.

Mama rested under
the tree, and Benjamin
zipped off to play.

Benjamin turned over rocks, looking for bugs....

He found a roly-poly bug that rolled into a ball when he touched it.

He saw crickets that chirped by rubbing their wings together. He saw an earthworm!

Then he saw something
jumping in the pond.
What could it be?
He crept closer to see
what was happening.

Lots of big, big fish!
I could catch one,
thought Benjamin.
He reached way out,
grabbing at the fish,
but they slipped away.

Then he saw a big whirligig.
It zipped right by him.
He tried to catch it.
But he reached too far and,
all of a sudden, *kersplash!!*
Benjamin was splashing
about in the pond.

His mama heard the *splash!* and ran faster and faster to see what was the matter!

Where was Benjamin?
She jumped in
to save Benjamin.
Splash!

Mama looked and looked,
but she couldn't see.
Just as she was about
to run out of breath,
she felt his nose.

Mama pulled Benjamin
out of the water.
All the pond critters
clapped and cheered for
Benjamin and his mama.
Yeah! Yippee!

Benjamin and his mama
shook off their wet fur.

Night was coming. Mama
picked up Benjamin and
carried him home.

Benjamin took
a hot bath,

put on his pajamas,

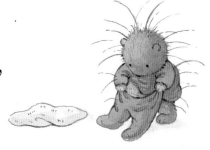

had a bedtime snack
of strawberries,

and brushed his teeth
and combed his fur.

Mama read Benjamin a bedtime story.
Then she kissed him good-night,
hugged him tight, and turned out the light.

butterfly   tadpole   snail   beetle   crawdad